My counters and cupboards were completely cleared of carrot cake, cornbread, and crackers.
BETTY'S BAKERY

This is a considerably crummy crime.

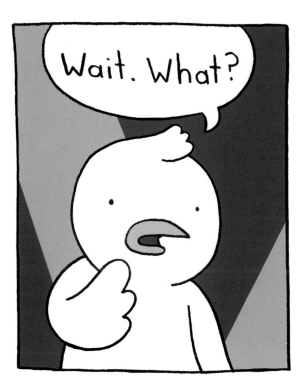

Betty, I'm no exhaustion expert, but you're extremely overextended.

Excuse me?

We'll explain explicitly.

Looks like we have our next mystery, team. LET'S GO!

The case of Betty's Burgled Bakery is closed! Now, can the world's greatest detectives solve this mystery of inconceivably hyperbolic hysteria?

STAY TUNED

Alliteration is the repetition of the same letter or sound at the beginning of multiple closely connected words. It's a device often used in poetry, prose, and songs to add all sorts of moods and feelings to what's being written.

You'll also find alliteration in cartoon character names, famous speeches, and even on cereal boxes. Look around! Alliteration abounds!

Consider adding alliteration to your writing. It can really **pack a punch**! Let's compare:

Peter Piper harvested two gallons of ripe tomatoes.

* Peter Piper picked a peck of pickled peppers.

BETTY'S BAKERY is HIRING HELP

Experience expected
Passion preferred

415

FREE FOOD FOR

Thanks, det
— Betty

Betty's Bakery
456 Apple Ave.

Pita	.49
Pumpernickel	.79
Pretzel	1.29
Total	**2.57**

Have a delightful day!

HUNGRY ANIMALS

PANDAS eat 20 to 40 pounds (9 to 18 kilograms) of bamboo each day and spend half of their lives foraging. They live in forests of their food. Can you imagine?!

BLUE WHALES are the largest animals that have ever lived, so of COURSE they have huge appetites. They eat almost 8,000 pounds (3,600 kilograms) of krill daily! Mmm . . . krill.

STAR-NOSED MOLES eat faster than any mammal on the planet. They find and swallow food as fast as you blink!

PYGMY SHREWS are the tiniest mammals, and they need to eat constantly to stay alive. They never sleep for more than a few minutes at a time!

HUMMINGBIRDS eat twice their body weight in nectar each day to feed their buzzing hearts and wings.

For Karina—my comrade, confidant,
and co-conspirator.

Library of Congress Cataloging-in-Publication Data available.

ISBN 978-1-4521-3183-2

Manufactured in China.

Design by Ryan Hayes.
Lettering by Travis Nichols.
The illustrations in this book were rendered in pencil on paper
and colored digitally.

10 9 8 7 6 5 4 3 2 1

Chronicle Books LLC
680 Second Street
San Francisco, California 94107

Chronicle Books—we see things differently. Become part of
our community at www.chroniclekids.com.